IF FIREFLIES TOLD TALES

FLASH FICTION

CINDY PEREIRA

Made with ♥ on the Notion Press Platform
www.notionpress.com

Contents

1. Mother Ocean — 1

2. Mirror, Mirror On The Wall — 3

3. Help! — 6

4. Lessons From A Dragonfly — 8

5. Tony — 9

6. Love Is A Ribbon In Pink And Blue — 12

7. Fifty Roses Each — 13

8. The Music Of Dust — 15

9. Old Soldiers And Chirping Birds — 16

10. No Turning Back — 17

11. The Folly In Fishing — 18

12. Once Twice Over — 21

13. As Good As New Again — 22

14. A Walk Among The Stones — 24

15. Like Mother Like Daughter — 26

16. Walking The Wall — 28

17. Project Dracula — 29

18. Maid To Order — 31

19. Kayoed — 33

20. A Farewell On The Wind — 34

21. Bella — 38

22. Guns And Roses — 40

23. Talking The Walk — 43

24. Another Fellow Sufferer — 45

Contents

25. The Proof Is In The Fire — 47

26. A Recipe For Love — 49

27. The Jungle Jury — 50

28. Captain Crawley — 53

29. Hope Floats — 55

30. A Taste Of Space — 56

31. Peach Plumish — 58

32. Five Minutes — 61

33. Waiting For Dragonflies — 62

34. A Prairie Butterfly — 63

35. Taking Out The Garbage — 65

36. Laugh And Forget — 67

37. Weekly Visit — 68

38. Pussycat Socks — 69

39. PS – Goodbye — 70

40. Domestic Clash — 72

About the Author — 75

1

Mother Ocean

Despite the debris that the ocean had hauled up all around, the beach felt therapeutic under her toes.

Across the aqua-blue expanse, the horizon was ablaze with the setting sun, and seagulls called over the eternal rush of the waves. Sometimes, the tidal foam touched her feet and receded, and the shoreline appeared to slide backwards.

She hated the unending expanse before her now. Like a shimmering leviathan rumbling within its belly, sometimes screaming, sometimes dreaming, but never silent, never still, it tossed and churned in waves of guilt. Out there, over that darkening line, she had lost everything, snatched to the depths by the force of this fiend.

Beyond the shoreline, where the town was winking ablaze with a million lights under the night sky, two children waited, bug-eyed and hungry. Children orphaned twice now – once when that shapeless expanse had snatched their father away, and now, when they lost the young man who had stepped in to take his place.

"You sure you want to go, Mick?" she had asked him for the hundredth time that day. "I heard the forecast is not too good."

"If I don't go, I don't get paid," he had replied. "And if I don't get paid, we don't eat."

Mick had always loved the ocean. He'd speak of the vast blue swell like it was a real person, a mother with a heart of gold heaving within her wide bosom.

So, he left in his yellow oilskins, hauling his bag over his shoulder and kissing the little ones and her goodbye.

It was a week today, and they had finally called off searching the rumbling ocean. They had come to her door, like they had done for the others, sliding their hats off and shaking their heads in silence. Numb and robbed, she had left the little ones to wander the shore and look upon her shifting nemesis for a while.

All at once, there was darkness. The fire on the horizon had gone, leaving only a red remnant upon the sky where the sun had struggled seconds ago. She gasped at the blackness, broken only by the flashes of the waves; like frills on a gigantic mother's cap, they rolled and fragmented to lace upon the beach.

Mick had gone, like that setting sun, extinguished by the ocean. Nothing remained except a tagline here and a mast there, a mute testimony to the unflinching fury of the seas. He had been all she had, but for the two little ones, now bewildered in their cribs, awaiting her return. He had been a part of her, emerging from her womb through sweat and tears. She remembered how she sighed in relief and laughed joyfully at his first lusty cry.

The forbidding ocean raced to touch her feet and shrank back, almost guilty of maternal treason. Heaving like a mighty mother, it moaned a lullaby for her own boy, now buried deep within that watery tomb.

2

Mirror, Mirror on the Wall

"Mirror, mirror on the wall, who is the most beaten of us all," mused Kevin, glancing once at his reflection. Today, he tried to ignore the bluish bruise on his cheek. He was shaved clean, his hair was gelled to perfection, and he was suited as slickly as a man ready to walk down the aisle.

Only it wasn't his wedding. He was meeting his wife Sylvia for their anniversary dinner. Under his spotlessly white shirt, ironed neat and crisp, his ribs still hurt. Beneath the shoulder pads of his smart navy-blue suit, the skin on his collarbone felt a little sensitive – like the tail end of a belt had ripped him there. The recollection of the pain had dulled. Kevin knew it would dissolve to nothing in time, but the mirror sometimes brought memories of old wounds.

The mark on his cheek was new. So was the throbbing ache in his heart, the raw feeling in his throat and the pain of shattered self-esteem.

He didn't like his reflection these days. He always encountered a bruised man staring back at him – a battered man – perhaps even a beaten man. Two months ago, he had a nasty bleeding nose, broken from a terrible fight. It had healed wonderfully on the surface, but he knew if he peered hard enough at his face, he'd see blood, pulp, and swelling.

The memory brought a swarm of tears, and he swallowed hard. Inhaling deeply, he gritted to himself, "You got this. It's going to be okay."

Taking one last glance at himself, he settled his tie and breathed deeply. Sylvia was going to look stunning, as usual, today. And she was going to make an entrance like a movie star, stepping elegantly out of a chauffeur-driven car and gliding up the steps of the restaurant to an impassive doorkeeper with a giant turban, bowing low in stoical welcome.

Kevin only hoped she'd like the gift he had got for her.

The table at the restaurant was in a cosy corner with perfectly romantic lighting overhead. Kevin reached into his pocket, feeling the tiny velvet box that contained a tasteful pair of earrings he had worked hard to buy. When his wife sailed in, radiant in red, he sucked in a deep breath with a pang of love. Remarkably, the bruise on his face didn't hurt so much now. It was just the mirror that told him tales, he thought with kindness.

He kissed her gently, and they sat down to chardonnay ruddy in crystal wine glasses. Smiling broadly, he slid the box towards her.

"Really?" she asked bright-eyed when she picked it up. "Kevin, don't tell me they're diamonds because I know you can't afford them. But, before anything, I must show you what Daddy got me for our anniversary..."

Excitedly, she reached into her handbag.

His dignity hurtled into the dust like a blow slugging his jaw. He swallowed his pride bitterly and looked away – another bruise, another scar.

Mirror, mirror on the wall....

3

Doug scratched his head at the algebra sum.

Noticing his friend, two desks up, wholly absorbed in its solution, he hissed desperately, "Becky!"

Another girl immediately in front snapped around instead, parting her lips over two racks of steel clips. Doug grimaced at the metal mouth and nearly swore. Why was she always seeking his attention?

"I can help," the girl whispered adoringly. "I'm good at this."

Doug rolled his eyes. "No, thank you, Metallica," he growled.

Ahead, the teacher nosed the air, and his bark for silence had the desired effect. The girl stuck her tongue out and snapped back to her algebra sum.

Doug gaped at Becky's back frantically. He knew she had all the answers to the muddling sum. Tearing off a slip of paper, he wrote 'help' in bold, rolled and bent it into a tight V shape. Then he caught a rubber band between the ends of the V and, with expert fingers, readied it for launch.

"Becky!" he seethed again, releasing his missile. Unluckily, his admirer turned around again, and the paper warhead shot across her face, snicking her nose.

"You could have taken my eye out with that," she gasped, shattering the silence of the classroom and hurling the dozing pedagogue from his pulpit.

Besides earning more algebra sums as atonement, Doug also had Metallica's company in detention that day.

"I thought love letters contained sweet words," she gushed into his groaning face. "But 'help,' by no means, is a bad start!"

4

Lessons From a Dragonfly

He fixed his eyes unseeingly ahead. The skyscrapers and traffic were indifferent.

When he stepped forward, a dragonfly rested on his shoe. A rainbow glimmered on its wings.

Giving up so soon?

Thoughtfully, he moved back from the building edge.

Perhaps next year, if he failed again.

But not now.

5

Tony

Gina opened her mouth to ask her boy where he'd been all day. But she sighed, looked towards heaven and shook her white head. A pointless exercise, she thought. Still, Tony was back home now, and that was all that mattered. Though gangling and hairy, like an awkward adolescent who had just begun to sprout manhood, he had the mind of a two-month-old! His entire vocabulary included only grunts, groans and growls. There were occasional howls and whines when he wanted to be facetious, but never words or sentences.

She had done all she could to raise and care for his every need. She and he would take walks in the park every evening – an odd couple rambling beside each other till the sunset swallowed up their long shadows – and then they would point their footsteps home.

Tony had been her daughter's little boy...but caring for one such as him had been difficult, and the girl had been a junkie. Then she packed her things one morning, years ago and left, never to return.

Now, Gina quickly glanced left and right and dragged a stubborn Tony past her door. She had to be vigilant, she realised with a pang of apprehension, and make sure she kept a watchful eye on him. He was always bound to wander, forget the time and stay out long in the dark until some trigger in his brain helped him find his way home again.

Sometimes, the neighbours complained when they found him in their garden patch, lying stupidly among the flowers, staring up at the sky, baring his teeth in a perpetual grin, his brown eyes almost mad and filled with challenge.

"Tie him up," they'd say callously as if he was some wild animal. "That way, he cannot wander."

But he had done just that today; he had wandered away even before she had risen in the morning and had stayed out all day. Gina had bitten her nails in panic. What if the agency found out that she could hardly control him anymore and took him away? She was too old now to care for him...but after all these years, Gina knew she could never live without her boy.

Still, he was home now, and she was relieved. She gently pulled his ear and asked:

"Where did you go, you naughty boy?"

Tony glanced at her, his big, brown eyes shining, and eagerly darted to the door.

Gina sighed. It didn't matter that he had been out the whole day. It was evening, and evening time meant the usual walks.

"Alright," she said with indulgent resignation.

Tony danced, tried to smile, and his tongue lolled out, oozing dribble. With eager anticipation, he cocked his head to one side and watched her don her coat. But when she reached for his collar and leash, he broke into delighted yowls and barks and bounded forward to be properly shackled.

And then they set out, an old woman and her dog.

6

Love is a Ribbon in Pink and Blue

Mary saw nothing else but her baby son. His closed eyelids were delicate and transparent, his parted lips like petals. His chest fluttered like a flower, bobbing in the rain.

But love also meant letting go. Kissing his little toes, she consented and broke down.

The doctor pulled the plug.

7

Fifty Roses Each

————◆♡◆————

Nicky felt the cold morning sun tingle on her back. She sat upon an old bench under a tree in the desolate garden, sipping a cup of coffee and thinking. The tree made dappled shadows on her dry, cracked feet, and she sighed deeply. It had been a challenging year. Her father had died in August, her mother just three months later, and tomorrow, she would turn 50 years old.

Both are in a better place; her friends' platitudes after the last funeral made her want to throw up. *As hard as we might sound, all their years of suffering are now behind you. You can get back on your feet, dye your hair, get a massage, and plan a holiday. You can live and love again.*

Really? Was it that easy?

Well, she told herself, grimacing at her cracked, painful heels and stubby toenails. *Platitudes or not, I can start with my feet, at least. The pain kills me when I walk!*

Her coffee had now gone cold, and with waning interest in it, she rose with a deep sigh of fatigue. What did she show for 50 years of her life? Greying hair, sagging cheeks, flabby tummy, and ugly, painful feet – the remnants of a long, hard battle. More than anything else, it had been a battle of immature denial that her parents could never fall sick and die. But they did; their lives had been long but fraught with pain and suffering. Nicky's nose reddened at the memory, and she gritted, trying to fight back the rawness of their passing so quickly between each other. Still, as tears smarted the back of her eyes, she smiled painfully.

"Talk about true love," she whispered.

Breathing deeply and taking control of herself, she looked up at the sky. It was chill, but the deep blue above was bright and cheerful. She could be happy too, she realised, if she gave herself a chance and perhaps heeded those stale words of comfort. A quick pedicure would be just the tick. And maybe tomorrow, she'd treat herself to a massage and a spa, buy a holiday package and enrol herself at the local gym.

Nicky set out early the following day, conscious of her soft pink feet perfectly shod in sandals that enhanced her finely shaped toenails. Her heels still pricked a little because of the cold cracks, but they were now soft and creamy. A light breeze blew into her face, tossing her greying curls about. She had an appointment with the spa, a movie ticket, and a massive shopping list.

But first things first, she told herself firmly.

Cradling two bouquets of 50 red roses each, Nicky sombrely entered a cemetery and placed them on a pair of fresh mounds of earth lying side-by-side. Beneath the sod lay resting the two people who had given her life half a century ago, and she bowed her head in silent thanks.

Then she turned to face what life now had to offer.

8

The Music of Dust

They lowered the casket into the green, and she watched. Their handfuls of dust played music on the wood, and she danced, liberated, limitless. They refused to cry; instead, they smiled because she was beyond all pain.

She bid them farewell – a tear, a smile and a rush of peace.

9

Old Soldiers and Chirping Birds

Dad had been paralysed.

Yet he flashed fiercely independent eyes upon his caregivers. Stubborn – almost mulish, he'd refuse their assistance, hobbling about on one leg.

"I'm a soldier," he'd say.

A second stroke finally took him down.

The birds chirped at his funeral, reminding us that *now* he was free.

10

No Turning Back

"Howdy schmecker!" someone sneered at him.

As I fought him and lost, I was yanked up and shoved into the sunlight.

"Don't be shy..." they heckled, but he didn't turn. Never would.

I was hurled into a car and driven to rehabilitation.

He's my brother. A one-time junkie, but clean now.

11
The Folly in Fishing

How could a man be such an idiot? Gary scratched his chin anxiously. Girls were hardly interested in fishing. They preferred dancing or shopping and certainly not pondering over water and taking in flora and fauna. Especially girls from the big cities, he mused uncomfortably.

Still, he and Emily had been friends as children, and fishing had been a favourite pastime. But Gary thought irritably, that was eight years ago. Now, she was a hot-shot lawyer in the city. What was he? A grimy farmer, his dad's successor, with a small patch of land. How could he match up to someone as accomplished as Emily? Besides, she now had a super-smart boyfriend, another dazzling councillor, and it seemed they couldn't get enough of each other.

He glanced across to her from where he sat and noted the rise and fall of her shoulders.

"Boring?" he asked with a sinking heart.

"No. I love to fish," came her instant response. "But there's not even a bite today. And you've caught at least five until now."

"They like me."

Emily made a face. "My bait is from the same tin as yours; I'm sitting in nearly the same place and not a bite," she moaned. "It's not like I've never fished before."

"Well, if you asked me," Gary began facetiously, "they're scared you might sue them for not tasting good enough."

"You're an idiot."

"That I am," he sighed. "I should have taken you dancing instead."

"I love to fish!" Her eyes shone. "Who cares about dancing?"

At that moment, a tall, smart-looking, slick-faced man stepped into the clearing, and Emily flew into his arms.

"Leroy! Where have you been? I missed you!"

Gary wrinkled his nose at the couple, now engaging in light intimacy. He turned away awkwardly. Then, as his eyes fell on the unattended fishing rod, an idea came to him. He quickly retrieved a fish from his catch, hooked it to the end of Emily's line and pitched it back into the water.

"Em!" he cried. "Your line!"

With a shriek of joy, she turned, lunged for her rod and triumphantly yanked a near-limp fish from the water.

"I caught one at last! Leroy! Gary! I caught one at last," she whooped.

"And deprived it of its life," Leroy grunted as Gary disengaged the fish from the hook. "Look! It's even lost the will to fight."

Emily's jubilant smile vanished. With a cry of pity and with no hesitation, she snatched the fish from Gary's hand and threw it back into the water.

"I sentence you to life," she declared as Gary cried out, astonished.

A smug-faced Leroy tugged at her hand. "Come," he said. "I heard this town has a dance floor. Let's go!"

Without even a glance at Gary, Emily and her boyfriend disappeared, their giggles ringing in his ears.

Sitting by the water, Gary hung his head dejectedly. A grimy farmer and a hot-shot lawyer? How could a man be such an idiot?

12

Once Twice Over

We have identical twin boys.

Bath time is fun but backbreaking because our basin is too small. So, the boys splash in turns.

Today, on round two, my second twin stormed and protested. I panicked. Was he in pain?

Then, that 'oh-oh' moment for a little man bathed twice over.

13

As Good as New Again

What a cacophony of varying pitches!

I settle on the couch with my fruit drink and watch the girls one by one. Though a little breathless, I don't worry too much about it. I know I'll be as good as new again by morning.

Fifteen of us waltz around this hall of food, music, dancing, and memories.

Ashley is by the buffet. She's still rotund from when we were little kids, clutching our food trays in the cafeteria. Now, she pecks at everything. Three or four times!

"Only tasting," she laughs when two other friends remark about the contents of her plate. "I must watch my weight. Who wouldn't want to look like Melanie?"

Melanie is behind me by the drinks. Her voice is modulated, and she has five devoted ladies orbiting her. Dressed like a movie star in a body-hugging tube gown that shows off her well-toned curves, she waxes about her elaborate workout regime. Well, I think to myself with a smile. I, too, might benefit from her advice, but I need something other than an exercise schedule these days.

"Now Charlie doesn't need to try," Melanie comments cheerfully to her fans. "She was always sporty back then in school. But we? We must work at it. Keep that sweat flowing to keep our faces glowing."

The five titter adorningly at the poetic attempt.

Charlie is on the other side of the hall. Her short skirt shows off legs that were once, and still are, the pride of a football field. She has no exercise routine other than to coach the sport she loves so much. She holds a glass of something. I can't discern what it is from where I'm seated, but her tiny, measured sips tell me it must be alcohol.

"Come on!" I hear her loud peal of laughter as she chats with another classmate. "I wasn't the skinniest in school, was I? What about little Minnie? We always joked that If she turned sideways, she'd disappear."

Minnie sits on a couch, out of earshot. Still so thin, she looks like one of those fashionable paper dolls we played with as children. Two other ladies sit with her, sharing their stories and talking in low voices. Then, one by one, they turn slowly and glance awkwardly at me, shaking their heads and sighing.

Later that night, in my night clothes, I tighten a belt around my left arm. Scar tissue glares at me where the blue artery now pulsates. Still, the needle doesn't waver in my hand – I've been doing this for years.

A familiar prick brings on a dull feeling of oedema. It's normal. This is my routine every other night. Connecting a thin tube to the needle, I watch my blood shoot through like a tiny black train in a tunnel. I lie down, and the beeps from the Nocturnal Home Haemodialysis Machine are like a lullaby.

By morning, the dialyser would filter my blood, and I'll be as good as new again.

14

A Walk Among the Stones

It's summer, but it's quiet.

I pick my way with care. I don't want to trample a flower or hurt a leaf – not even a weed. Over the lichen-coated wall, the traffic races left and right, and the sky seems stricken with emphysema.

But here, under the exuberant May trees, blazing like fire, the blue above is remarkable, and the clouds are like feathers. It's so quiet I can hear the hum of a bee poking around in casks of pollen, carrying messages from blossom to blossom. The sun glints through dappled shadows on every stone I pass like fairies dancing on silent floors.

There are stones carved with dates and names, some with verses, some with words, some with poems, and some with stories.

I have mine, too.

"You've gone through a pack!"

"That's nothing for me."

"But the doctor...?"

"I give a damn about the doctor!"

"Aren't you worried?"

"About what?"

"Your lungs!"

He laughed into my worried face. His throat seemed to splutter into coughing, like bubbles rupturing in a tube.

Still, a lighter clicked, a flame flickered, and the cherry end of a cigarette glowed like the blazing May Flower he now lies under.

The bee sings distantly, high on pollen, and a ladybug conquers a blade of grass. There's a song on the breeze as it shivers through the leaves.

And the summer sun dapples on his tombstone like fairies dancing on silent floors.

15
Like Mother Like Daughter

"You're harbouring another rapist!" cried my mother indignantly.

"And you're harbouring thoughts of murder." My reply was calm.

"Why are you so stubborn?"

"The law convicted his father, not him!"

"Like father, like son!" Mother's eyes were boiling with rage. If looks could burn, I would have been a lump of ash by now. But then, like mother, like daughter too - at least in some ways. I dug my heels in.

"You're not making sense!" I sighed. "If what you say is true, why didn't I end up like you?"

Mother had a fine backhand, catching me right below my jaw. Of course, she needed to be tough. She ran the "Swinging Girls" with an innuendo for a tagline, "Come one, come all," and I was the outcome of a romp that had paid well.

But then, I was tough, too. I wasn't a Swinging Girl – still, the business had sent me to college. It certainly got me to drop out when a shadow man forced his way into our home a few months ago. The memory was horrifying, but I wasn't going to give in. The boy was going to stay!

"You're going to beat me now?"

"I will not have him living under my roof and eating at my table!" Mother seethed.

"Fine with me."

Packing my clothes, I shouldered past her. "I'll be in touch."

My mother raised me alone. I could do the same, too.

I walked out, holding my growing baby bump.

16

Walking the Wall

The endless white, undulating, rising haphazardly to peaks of jagged black. Above, the deep azure sky.

Harsh, freezing country – harsher still the rat-tat-tat of an assault rifle. The ice reddened sluggishly. A grim soldier lowered his weapon.

"Over my dead body, pig!" he spat.

One infiltrator down, many to go.

17

Project Dracula

My tongue worked non-stop, and no, I wasn't talking. Not this time, at least. I was on a mission to earn some bucks from the Tooth Fairy.

To put it plainly, I now used my clapper as an effective irritant to further loosen my second front tooth. Last week, I'd swallowed my first and had had horrible dreams of another mouth growing in my tummy!

My chomper now hinged forward, and the exquisite pain got me yearning for more. To counter the effects of that sweet agony, I worked my tongue the other way. Then came an idea! What if I twisted it? So, I marched to the mirror and said, "Eeeee."

Touching the renegade fang gingerly, I rotated it. The pain stung and flowered on the adjacent tooth.

"Ooh! Salty," I slurped. "Dracula!"

That was the seed crystal!

Tying one end of a string to my dangling incisor, I fastened the other end to the doorknob. Closing my eyes, I breathed deeply and jerked my head backwards. Searing pain, a spatter of blood, but a welcome dental clink as ivory ricocheted off the door!

Proudly snapping my gaping and bloody gums into the mirror, I said with an air, "*I am Dracula. And I bid you welcome.*"

The elder sibling didn't think so. A deriding guffaw followed his expert opinion:

"You can get a bus through there!"

I'm placing my tooth under his pillow tonight, hoping Dracula, not the gentle Tooth Fairy, comes to visit!

18
Maid to Order

The maid shuffled about in Martha's kitchen, singing as she worked.

Martha tried to hum along but found it difficult. She didn't know Cantonese. Besides, she had a guest, her son, Neil, who was meeting her for the first time in two years!

"Would you like some tea, Martha?" the maid's accentuated voice called, breaking from the song. "Does Neil drink tea?"

"Yes, he does. And thank you, Dear." Martha smiled at Neil's astonished face.

With Tina taking care of her now, she didn't miss her son too much. He was a busy man. Too busy, she mused with a sigh.

"You have a maid!" he exclaimed unnecessarily. "Anyway, how have you been, old girl?" He didn't wait for a response. "You know how it is. Work, work, work. They've made me partner, Mum!"

"How nice."

When Tina brought the snacks, Neil observed her with interest.

She was young, fresh, and pink, with almost transparent eyelids. She mixed the tea with supple and perfect hands and handed them their cups. Neil smiled at her, hoping to get familiar. Tina's returning smile never touched her black, expressionless eyes or even creased the skin on her alabaster face.

Neil gaped and wondered what was odd.

Then it hit him, and he froze.

"Mum!" he gasped. "Is that a....?"

Martha chuckled. "It's life, Jim, but not as we know it," she quoted philosophically and sipped her tea.

In the kitchen, Tina resumed her song in Cantonese.

19

Kayoed

My wife's a knockout!

For a whole five minutes, she stared into her excessive, extravagant wardrobe, weighing her options.

Then, sighing in boredom, she donned an old T-shirt and faded jeans.

"What the...?" I was flabbergasted.

"I've nothing else to wear," came her petulant explanation.

I'm still trying to recover!

20

A Farewell on the Wind

When Lilly jumped, the belt of her dress snared on the balcony grill, and she hung in mid-air, screaming for help!

Her life flashed before her eyes. Childhood, adolescence, adulthood, marriage ... death.

Two weeks ago, Michael had come home from work, showered, shaved, written a farewell note to her, and jumped thirty floors off the balcony!

Now, she sobbed at the memory. Why? Why?

Under the bright afternoon sky, fluffy clouds sailed a sea of blue, and Michael seemed to call to her. Hanging thirty stories high, Lilly, clinging to precious life, only cried out as if in response to his grizzly invitation:

"No! No!"

The wind whipped around her, and a little paper fluttered away from the balcony like her soul in flight. She wept, screamed, and realised with a sudden desire to live that she didn't want to die like Michael. What he had done made no sense. They had been happy – childless, yes, and high-strung at work. But still happy. Happier than many couples their age.

Glancing up again, Lilly glimpsed a sturdy iron rail two inches above – the balcony. She reached up but clutched only air. She was hanging by her belt and facing outwards. Heaving herself upwards and backwards was next to impossible. It needed a backward pull-up; she could barely manage one the usual way without gasping and stopping to rest. All she could do was holler for help! It was a working day, and her neighbours in the adjoining flats were out. Thirty stories high, all was silent, and Lilly was alone.

"Let go, Lilly," she thought when Michael's memory returned, and, for only an instant, giving up seemed so appealing. "He's only seconds away."

Even so, one downward glance turned her blood cold. The belt, tight around her waist, gave weird comfort. But it cut into her skin, too, and agonised her. Instinctively, she shifted to relieve the tension, and it slipped up suddenly, catching beneath her ribcage. She shrieked again, flailed her arms and began to sweat. A fall was a long way down! They had found Michael splattered in blood, broken and mangled. The memory drove her nauseous. It also beckoned. What did she have to live for now? Michael was gone, and she didn't want to be alone. But hurtling downward filled her with dread, too. She could never flutter away like her farewell note. She'd have to succumb to the force of gravity to pass into Michael's realm, and death would be cruel!

"I'm sorry, Michael," she sobbed and fought to turn around, to face away from the dizzying world. "I love you, but I want to live."

The action only hurt more. The belt, taut, held her securely but allowed no other movement. She could only reach back and grasp some part of it, but not the balcony. She tried once, twice, three times, and only clawed at the air. Lilly cried and gnashed in frustration.

"You can do this," she gritted. "Focus. Focus."

Reflexively, she looked down, and the depts turned her dizzy. "Oh God!" she cried. "Look up! Look up! Focus!"

Breathing deeply and out through her lips repeatedly, Lilly fought to stay calm.

"As long as you're alive, there's hope," she consoled herself and pursed her lips. Then, with a supreme effort, she twisted her body around, managing a partial turn.

"You can do this! You can do this," she seethed and twisted again. The belt slipped up at that moment, catching her under her armpits. Her brief downward plummet pumped blood into her knees and almost paralysed her.

"Help!" she shrieked. "Help me! Oh God! Somebody help me!"

She was still ensnared by her belt but in deadly peril now. If she reached up, she would slip through the loop and go ... down ... down ... down ... down.

How would it be, she wondered and sobbed in that fleeting instant of horror. Did Michael see the ground surge up to meet him, or did his heart go into arrest in the brief moments of his downward hurtle? Even as those thoughts flashed through her mind and Michael's mangled remains came back to her, she lunged one arm upwards to grasp the concrete ledge of the balcony.

It worked! Her fingers found a solid hold, and it felt cool and firm for that moment. Lilly sighed. Her belt still snared her precariously, but she managed to loop her other arm around the tight slack. It cut her skin, but the pain barely registered. Gasping, wheezing, she mustered her strength and lunged upwards herself again. In that second of horror, Lilly felt suspended in air, one arm tangled around her belt and impotent, the other clawing for the balcony rails.

Then she grasped metal, and her fingers held fast. The second upward heave loosened the slack a little, and she was able to clasp the rail with her other hand. She was going to pull herself up, she promised. But for now, she needed to rest and catch her breath.

Laughter and tears came together – grief for a dead husband and a relieved giggle for herself. The realisation that she could make it out of her ordeal was sweet – her second chance.

Her belt catching on the rails had been her first. If Michael had only given himself a chance...

Her farewell note was flying somewhere, but she was still alive, which made all the difference.

21
Bella

I don't like the fence between our homes. A long line of wooden slats extending from the front to the back, with not so much as even a chink where I can peep and watch her play.

Yes, she'd play. How often, while sitting on the porch, I would see that ball rise high from the pool and hear yells of encouragement from her family.

"Go, Bella," they'd hoot. "Take that header, girl."

I don't like yelling, but I think Bella would do well in football. Who would take her in their team, though?

If I were a coach, I would!

But I'm not. I find it difficult to communicate with my own family. Or even relate to them. They are unlike me. They understand the world differently. I wish they'd recognise that I'd love to have a friend like Bella.

It's Friday evening today, and it's been a hot day. Nothing's been right. My tutor was somewhat annoying, too, coaxing me to do stuff that made no sense to me. Different from my routine!

Even Bella has been silent.

I toddle over to the fence between our homes to try and peep through. A slat is pushed forward, and the wood has a hole. Suddenly, a moist, black beetle appears there – it takes me a moment to realise it's a snout. The slat pushes even further, and I see a velvet-black head with deep brown eyes.

I reach out, and a pink tongue greets my hand.

Bella.

22
Guns and Roses

"Excuse me, please."

The voice was strident but dripping with juvenile arrogance and mockery. Rose, who had stepped down from the buckboard, turned around, her black eyes smiling – but that turned into confusion an instant later.

"Yes?" she said in a soft, mellow tone, aware that her class of rumbling children had gathered at the door and windows in the small school building ahead. Some of the townspeople had stopped to stare in interest, too.

"Yes," mimicked the owner of that voice, a lanky lad with a freckled face and a pugnacious nose. "Your kind ain't welcome here, woman," he added.

She raised her brows. She thought she probably was double the boy's age, but Rose didn't want to lock horns with Bubba Pardue, the son of one of the wealthiest cattlemen around. So, she smiled again and parted her lips to reply to him when a low voice from the school porch cut in:

"An' what kind would that be, kid?"

The boy glanced around the lady at a figure lounging in a chair. This was a dark-haired man with long legs stretching languidly out. The bronzed face was boyish, pleasant and friendly, but there was nothing amiable about the crossed cartridge belts and the low-tied twin guns strapped to his supple hips.

Bubba dismissed it as a bluff and said haughtily:

"Dunno how you'd be concerned, but since you're interested, the colour of her skin ain't exactly like mine. Darkies are meant to be slaves, not teachers."

"I think he needs some education," mused the stranger aloud. "Mebbe he ain't aware that the Confederacy collapsed and slavery is abolished."

His eyes crinkled into a smile when he turned to Rose. "Ma'am," he said. "Don't let that ill-mannered kid hold you back."

Bubba's face twisted malevolently when Rose, with a bit of trepidation, stepped forward. He sprang in front of her, blocking her passage to the school.

"Uh-huh, Nigger," he sneered and roughly shoved her back.

It was all the movement the stranger needed. He strode down from the porch in four long strides, his spurs jingling on the wooden boards. With a sudden swing of his arm, he brought it down with a resounding slap on Bubba's cheek. The boy teetered, falling backwards in the dust.

With a howl of rage, Bubba reached for his gun. It was a clumsy movement, but he wasn't interested in the finesse of his draw. A killing rage had entered him, and he aimed for the back of the man who had now turned to help the teacher to her feet.

In that instant, she screamed in horror. The children and the crowd shrieked and cried out, too, and the stranger sensed something was amiss.

He swung around, but even as he moved, his six-gun materialised in his hand, and it was belching fire.

Bubba only felt the agony of a shattered forefinger as his gun clattered from his hand.

"I didn't miss," warned the stranger meaningly. Then he turned to Rose gallantly, and she accepted his proffered arm.

She stepped over the stunned boy and headed for the classroom.

23
Talking the Walk

"But-but-but…" he protested, and his fat, pink arms flapped in open rebellion. Obviously, he didn't care about my shopping bags!

"No buts," I hushed him, raising a warning finger to let him know I wasn't joking.

"But I don't wanna walk on my own," he whined, and I glared at him for the first time in all my life and his. Of course, he wouldn't want to walk on his own! Why? When he had that fancy 'walker' that took away the need to move his legs – me!

"You have two legs," I said firmly. "You know how to walk, so use them. I cannot help you all the time. How are you going to exercise your legs and make them strong? You'll be a cripple all your life. Do you want to be a cripple?"

He was hardly listening to me.

Flopped on the floor of the mall with people milling around us, he stared at me like I was some ogre refusing to help this rotund … person and refused to budge.

It was getting embarrassing! I spent my life crossing swords with my dad, who loved to make his mild stroke appear more serious than it really was.

Was history repeating?

Still, there he was, stagnated on the shiny mall floor, where a million shoes carrying a zillion germs had trod, arguing with me with his big brown eyes and bugs bunny smile.

I groaned, gave in and swung my toddler into my arms.

24
Another Fellow Sufferer

Stooping is not easy. I have to start thinking about it in the morning if I have to bend over by noon!

I wasn't always old and tattered. There was a time when I was young and strong, and Marie was like a flower in spring.

Those days, folks called me Luke the Lion because of my thick red hair and proud handlebar moustache. Then, the kids grew up and got too busy with their lives. Like tattered coats hanging behind the door, they left us to the moths.

Torn open, with our insides spilling out in silent tears, we resigned ourselves to our fate. Now we're numb, old and faded, stagnant in a place that stinks of age and decay.

The other relics here, fellow sufferers, sunken deep and dozing in their armchairs, don't know, don't remember and don't care for Luke the Lion.

Even Marie doesn't remember.

I shuffle away on shaky legs to escape the decay – an impossible task. Then, as I try to shake off the feeling, I see it.

On the side of the road, the discard of some child, a faded toy, stares blankly at the world.

I stoop and pick it up.
Another fellow sufferer!

25

The Proof is in the Fire

Cathy trembled when the police investigator shoved a loaded laundry stand aside. He suspected her son, Johnny, of murder and a search warrant stuck out of his pocket. The only thing was that the officer didn't have proof, and he and two other men ransacked her home, looking for clues.

Her son was now in police custody, but that could change in 48 hours if they didn't find evidence to pin him to the crime. A vicious mugger had attacked his pregnant wife, robbing him of his unborn child, and Johnny had hunted him down!

His wife now battled for life in the hospital.

The laundry stand tipped over and crashed to the floor. Lighting a cigarette, Cathy tried to remain calm. Johnny had slipped on the attacker's blood and had come home to clean up. If the police found trace evidence, her son was finished. Even under mitigating circumstances, he'd get life for premeditated murder!

"The man was a thief," she stated as the detectives upturned drawers and pulled down shelves. "Anyone could have battered him!"

"Suspicion points to your son, Mrs Jenkins," muttered the cop, frustrated that they came up with nothing. He and his partners turned to leave. "We'll be back," he added ominously.

Cathy waited till they were gone. Then she ferociously gathered the wash, especially the socks, where faint bloodstains were still visible. She lit a fire at the back and consigned everything to flames, waiting until the last piece of evidence turned to ash.

26

A Recipe for Love

You couldn't call it a fight. It was a storm! The kind accompanied by howling winds, without a drop of substance.

Their thunderous spat simmered in silence.

Two days.

Then she tried a recipe to liven her mood, and he mumbled that it was a hit.

Giggles, laughter and hugs!

27

The Jungle Jury

Inspector Dan Geoghegan watched impassively as the two prisoners alighted from the van. Their wrists were handcuffed to each other, and their faces bore the brutality of the interrogation they had been through sixteen hours before. They had stopped in the middle of nowhere – a ribbon of road stretching through a wild forest of massive trees, clumpy bamboo and prickly shrubs. The isolation was magnified by a red setting sun where the highway ran into the horizon.

Geoghegan gestured with his chin for them to get on with their business.

"This is the only stop for the next 300 miles," he warned as he lit a cigarette. "Swine like you will be happy to piss your pants, but I have a sensitive nose."

The prisoners, two young men with perpetual sneers despite the bruises, turned around and spread their feet to urinate in the bushes.

Geoghegan regarded them as he smoked. Two rapists. Two murderers. They had stalked a girl on her way home from work, cornered her in a dark spot, raped her and then butchered her. Their reason? A girl had no business being out so late! Now, they were in judicial custody, awaiting trial and were on their way to the prison.

Trial? What trial? It would take years before a conviction.

Having finished their ablutions, the men turned, sneering at the cop as if challenging him to shove them back into the van. Geoghegan sucked at his cigarette and wondered what their faces might look like if they had a single bone of remorse in their bodies. He couldn't form an image – their faces were mocking even from behind the curtain of smoke. They were a breed of men from Hell – predators entitled to a fair trial because the law of the land applied to both men and the two-legged variety of beasts! Geoghegan recalled the remains of the young girl. She had been viciously mauled and murdered because of their black ideology that likely never existed at any time!

"I'm thinking," he told them. "The forest is just as bad as any prison cell – 250 square miles of desolation and danger. With the night coming on, you have as good a chance here as you would have at the place you're going. Now," continued the laconic Inspector. "The law will take its time before it gets you, but those chaps in there? They have a weird sense of honour and no respect for rapists. Two hours, that's all. Two hours, and you'll find yourselves in the dispensary, getting your butt-holes working again."

For an instant, two pairs of eyes blinked. Then realisation dawned! It was the forest versus a prison cell, the wilderness versus brutality, the unknown versus bestiality. With a yell, they spun around and took off into the undergrowth.

Dan Geoghegan smiled and coolly palmed his handgun. Two rounds echoed in the blackening wilderness; then, there was silence.

Justice was served.

28

Captain Crawley

"Did you notice her skirts," hissed Ana to her sister. "Layers and layers of pinks and mauves. Who was she?"

"I don't care," replied Estelle shortly. "I only want to get home to Captain Crawley."

"Oh! You and your Captain Crawley!"

"And you and some silly girl's skirts! So what if the prince danced with her all night? I find him ugly and repulsive. Unlike my Captain Crawley!"

"You are mad," gasped Ana at the slur against Royal magnificence. "But just think, Estelle. A mysterious girl turns up in the most gorgeous dress, dances with our Prince and then rides away in a strange-looking carriage."

"Leaving behind a silly slipper," continued Estelle. "Disgraceful! Who does that?" Then she turned thoughtful. "But I agree with you. That horse's nose looked stubby. And the carriage? Like a giant golden egg."

"Almost as if a pug with a plume was pulling a pineapple," Ana breathed.

The play on words brought on peals of laughter in the carriage.

Back at home, in her attic room, their step-sister Ella frantically tried to hide one tiny glass slipper among her meagre possessions. She heard the carriage draw in and listened as the door opened. A wheezing growl sounded, followed by a confused exclamation.

"Captain Crawley!"

Ella padded down the stairs and peeped into the room. It was a strange sight. A large, yellow pineapple stood by the door, and beside it, staring at his mistress in absolute suspicion, was a pug – the handsome Captain Crawley.

29

Hope Floats

I remember the lake teeming with pink lotuses. The sky sweeping down to it was dazzling, and the sun was a divinely shattered diamond on its expanse. Only one eagle circled the blue, looking for prey in the sweep of the grasslands around.

Now, the verdant landscape is gone - lost to progress!

High above, a militia of eagles flaps in a dismal dome of deterioration. Like a decaying tooth, only grey and black abound as industry, high-rises, and pollution fill the lake.

Then I see it! One tiny pink lotus is holding out strong in the murky water.

Maybe there's hope?

30

A Taste of Space

"But what if I space out?"

Julie hissed the words, peering around her friend, Lisa, to make sure her mother was not entering her room.

"Really, Jul," came the disgusted reply. "You wanted it; believe me, pinching it off my dad was a task."

"I know, I know." Julie's thirteen-year-old face looked contrite. She bit her lip, glanced at her friend and then at the spoils of teenage pillage, and broke into a wild giggle. It was wrapped in brown paper and looked entirely innocent. "What if I get all ... you know what I mean?"

"Then soak your head under the shower," came Lisa's careless reply. "I've kept to my end of the bargain and, as you can see, I'm not in space ... yet."

Lisa was beginning to laugh, too, but she hushed instantly when Julie's mother called out, asking the girls if they were studying or reading Photo Romance comics!

"We are just getting to it, Mum," her friend lied. Then she giggled in silence again, slowly picking up the brown paper bag. "Gosh! What if I throw up?"

"I didn't."

"Are you already spaced out, Lisa?"

"I must be," came the flippant response. "I can see stars!"

Another burst of giggles followed. Then, with a deep breath of resolution, Julie delved into the bag, uncorked a bottle cap with a soft plop and took her first swig of Lisa's father's whiskey.

31

Peach Plumish

"Are you sure, Maddy?" asked Sheila, eyeing a tube of expensive lipstick. "Peach Plumish," she read the label. "You never liked Rowan. Now you're going dancing with him!"

"Come on! We were kids then," Maddy giggled. "He's become such a hunk!"

"He's also very successful and rich now."

Rowan, their friend from school, had bumped into Maddy a few months earlier and had rekindled their friendship. It had been nothing serious, but she hoped they'd begin dating soon. Back then, while in school, he'd been a poor boy whose father worked in a factory. Things had changed now, and Rowan had become a successful investment banker. Sooner or later, Maddy dreamed, he would go down on a knee and push a rock on her finger.

"I wouldn't have minded if he was still poor," Maddy murmured.

Sheila laughed, glancing at the lipstick. "Liar," she said. "That's why you gave him a hard time back then. Because he was poor."

"Not true!" Maddy gasped.

"True," insisted Sheila. "I remember he hankered after you like a puppy, and you broke his heart each time!"

"I didn't," Maddy replied crossly.

As she walked home from work that evening, she wondered about it. Rowan McCarthy had been the awkward little boy in school who yearned for her like most of the boys in her class. He'd bring her flowers from his mother's garden and gape in confusion as the posies were brutally binned.

"Gosh, McCarthy," she'd say in scorn. "I can't go around with every random guy!"

Now, he had grown up, done well for himself and was no more that poor ugly duckling—quite the opposite.

Besides, who didn't like a little wealth?

Maddy looked stunning on the night of the dance, and Peach Plumish had been worth every penny. Not only did it match her pink, flawless skin, but it also paired perfectly with her gown—a beautiful, deep-blue dress that clung to the contours of her body.

And Rowan clutched his heart when he came to pick her up. Mentally awarding full points to Peach Plumish, she revelled in his attention and blushed when he sought her exclusively for every dance. Then they took a break on the balcony, sipped champagne and looked up at the sky, whispering to each other.

"You look ravishing," he said as he held her, and she leaned back in his arms, hoping he'd bend and completely smudge her lipstick.

His cell phone rang instead, and he reached for it instantly. As he spoke into it, he walked a little away from her. Maddy sipped her drink, curiously trying to listen to his low conversation.

Had she not eve's-dropped, she might have been a happier woman that night. Sadly, she caught what he said and froze in indignation. Tearing up, she ran away, wiping her lipstick off.

It was demeaning to hear him guffaw and softly tell his caller:

"No, no. I'm here with some random chick. It's absolutely nothing serious at all."

32

Five Minutes

Roses in my arms. Five minutes in my mind.

"Please, let's talk, Mary," she pleaded. "Only five minutes."

"Leave," I cried. "With friends like you, who needs enemies?"

Squeezing my shoulder, she left. Then I heard the crash.

I follow her coffin, caressing roses and thinking of five measly minutes.

33

Waiting for Dragonflies

The traffic, two stories below, was like a regiment of steel shooting up and down the dusty road.

But for Stevie, pressed in earnest anticipation behind an enormous glass window, the movement below was like a shifting rainbow, like dragonflies gliding noiselessly in the sunlight.

He eagerly watched the cars, his mouth hanging open and his breath fogging the glass.

Then, breaking away from the regiment, one red car halted soundlessly in the drive. Even as the orphanage matron greeted them, Stevie shrieked delightfully and charged for his little suitcase.

He was going home to his new family at last.

34
A Prairie Butterfly

Dylan Conway established that his wife, Sally, had run away sometime in the night. She left him a note with her gold band and their marriage license.

In the soft light of dawn, as the horns and hooves of a thousand head of cattle started to move sluggishly across the prairie, Dylan surveyed the empty chuck-wagon, where he had left her crying the night before after their fight. He never thought she'd leave. It was twenty miles to Fort Worth, and she was afoot!

He had left his burnt-down house with one of his cowboys in Oklahoma. With his remaining riders and Sally, he had braved the 300-mile cattle drive south, across Apache Territory and the Red River, bound for Fort Worth, Texas. The army needed beef, and he needed the money to rebuild his home.

But Sally was his wife. True, only for the last three months, and that too because she had shown enough spirit one evening during a fight to make him pin her down and have his way with her. He married her because it was the right thing to do, but Ursula had always been his woman, and he had flung that to Sally's face last night.

Her big, beautiful, tear-laden eyes came back to him in a rush, and he blinked away the image with regret.

"*Dylan,*" her note read. "*You have no time for sentimentality, so I'll be quick.*

"*I'm leaving. Not because I was tired and dizzy in the afternoon today, and you wouldn't let me rest.*

"*I'm leaving because we've never had a marriage.*

"*I'll take half the blame for what happened between us. I could have stopped you, but I didn't. My reason is simple. I loved you – from the moment I saw you when Ursula brought me to the ranch as your housekeeper.*

"*I know you love her, yet you were forced to marry me because of one mistake. A forced marriage is null and void.*

"*Our marriage is a secret, and I promise it will continue to be. I'll leave you to make up a story of why your housekeeper left, but if I stayed, everything would soon be known, and I will not have it for your sake.*

"*I'm giving you back your ring and the proof that I am your wife.*

"*Do with it as you will. You're a free man now, my love.*

"*I hope you find the coward who burnt down the house.*"

Dylan glanced at his palm, where her band glittered in the morning sun. Then he gazed at her note, recalling her bright eyes, rosy cheeks, and sheer grit and determination on the drive. With an oath of admiration, he mounted up, spurring his horse towards the sea of cattle.

Fort Worth was twenty miles south, and the drive was almost over. But Dylan knew it wasn't done for him yet.

He had his wife to find and a ring to slip on her finger.

35

Taking Out the Garbage

Ronny Felder always had an eye for my daughter. She's only fourteen.

His father is a cabinet minister, so Ronny has grown horns and a tail. It's bad enough that he's a spoiled kid. At thirty, you'd think boys would settle into dignified manhood. It's all about exploitation with Ronny because he can hide behind his father's power.

Well, that was okay by me until he chose to bring his garbage past my door.

Now, his father, a hardline politician, has enemies – many are out to get him, and with two attempts already on his life, the Rt Hon Felder does not leave his home without maximum security.

Their house stands like a castle on a vast expanse of land, backed by forest and a hedge that separates their gamekeeper's home – mine – from themselves. Today, it looks black and forbidding against the snow. It would take a marksman with a high-powered rifle fitted with a telescope to get Felder.

One afternoon before Christmas, when I was out, Ronny barged past my door, dragged Millie from her books and ravaged her innocence.

Today is Christmas Day. I watch the family and their sentries gather by the cars to get to church. Well, Ronny has likely forgotten who Millie's dad is.

Tomorrow, the papers would say that another attempt was made on the Rt Hon Felder's life, that they missed but got his son instead.

Sounds good to me.

I part the hedge and take aim.

36

Laugh and Forget

You laugh like dew-dipped morning glories blooming on a hedge. As if you slept in sweet dreams of whispering angels.

Lucky you!

But then, I wonder how you can still laugh when you trashed my heart and strolled away with her?

Tell me! I want to laugh and forget, too.

37
Weekly Visit

Today, I'm spending time with school friends in a restaurant. They chatter proudly about their kids, and I think about mine. I get to visit him only once a week.

"My girl is eighteen," says one.

"I have two boys, and one is already married," another announces proudly.

I smile awkwardly but remain silent.

Later, after we say our goodbyes, I race to see him.

The place he's at is like a fort, and though I'm a little late, I know I can still make it.

I'm weary, but I'll still get to see my son and talk to him with a glass wall between us while a stoic policeman stands guard.

38
Pussycat Socks

It's chill, so I slip on your pink pussycat socks. You last wore them in the hospital. You loved them – cats, I mean. Now, you walk with them in light; all those you couldn't save – little furballs wrapping around your ankles and keeping you warm.

I only have your socks.

39

PS — Goodbye

Remember when we argued because you brought your stinky boots into the tent? You were petrified of centipedes crawling into them to keep warm. Centipedes have noses, too, my brother! The shoes are still in your room. Mum cleaned them and left them in your usual place under the bed.

She wants nothing changed.

By the way, I've washed the photographs you took with Grandad's camera. The pictures of our camp are pretty good considering the gadget's ancient. I had to read up on how to work with film roll. In some of the snaps, Mum says it's impossible to tell us apart.

No one could. I guess it's the same with all identical twins.

I'm wearing the tie you gifted me on our birthday. I should be wearing black like Dad, but I'd rather wear this than anything else. He helped me with the knot and nodded as if to tell me everything would be okay.

Would it?

You left a note for me under a writing pad in your room. Sally, who refused to be here today, demanded I burn it. It's not something to remember, she says. Well, you know how big sisters are.

I know she'll turn up soon.

You always had an eye for my Zippo! I recall how you'd casually pocket it after we lit up, hoping I'd not notice. Mum, Dad and Sally don't know, but I slipped it beside you in the coffin.

It's yours now.

40
Domestic Clash

Simon rolled his eyes, abandoned his dinner and paced upstairs to his room. He'd heard his mother open the front door and exclaim:

"Oh, Fred! Thank Goodness you're home. I was getting worried again."

The door closed with a click, and his mother began to grouse:

"Why do you do this to me, Fred? Why?" Shuffling sounds reached Simon's ears. His mother had now moved to the kitchen to putter around. "You have no regard for your wife or your son? See, he's now left his dinner untouched."

Like low death rattles, more grumbles funnelled up the stairs to his room. Shuffling feet clapped in soft rubber slippers told a tale of a woman high-strung and fickle in her actions. Simon clenched his fists, resisting the temptation to charge downstairs and put an end to the constant natter. It irritated him because once it started, it ended badly.

It also frightened him.

He shuddered, sat on the edge of his bed and cradled his head. Rocking himself, he tried to calm down as the grumbling persisted, rising in volume and accompanied by vessels skidding around on the counter. Soon, there would be havoc, and the kitchen would be a mess—he'd only just cleaned up an hour ago when she had driven him crazy, wondering where his father was.

Were the drugs working? Apparently not!

Downstairs, the whining increased in intensity; like the crescendo of a rising desert wind, it began to howl through the rooms. Feet began to tread heavily as they scampered this way and that. A drawer slammed open, and Simon heard the contents crash to the floor.

"You don't care anymore!" his distraught mother wailed. "You've changed over the last six months! You left the house at dawn today, and look at the time you've returned! It's close to midnight, Fred! We are supposed to be a family—you, me, and that young man who left his food untouched because of your selfish nature. Stop gaping at me as if I'm crazy! I could gouge your eyes out, you horrible, horrible man!"

A crash sounded like breaking glass, followed by a piercing scream. Simon sprang up in alarm and raced downstairs. When he entered the kitchen, he groaned in dismay. A drawer of silverware lay overturned on the floor. A dish of food was splattered across the kitchen top, and a glass pane from one of the cabinets had shattered. But crumpled in a corner, his mother lay, nursing her bleeding heel, trying to dislodge a shard she had trampled on when she smashed the glass.

"Mum, you've got to stop this!" he cried, falling at her feet.

"Stop what?" she asked, extracting the glass from her heel. Simon pressed a napkin over the bleeding gash and glared into her bewildered face.

"Stop imagining Dad's still here with us," he gritted. "He's been dead six months now, and you're freaking me out!"

He shook his mother's shoulders and broke down helplessly by her side.

About The Author

Cindy Pereira, born and raised in Bangalore, India, prefers to be called a storyteller rather than a writer. Her love for making up stories began at a very young age when her dolls became the actors for scripts written in her mind. This turned to writing in middle school when she and her best friend hand-wrote stories for each other, complete with binding and cover pages. Some of her stories spark from actual life events, and some are just yarns.

She loves to participate in short story competitions and won first place in the short story segment of Lockdown Diaries (organised by Secure Giving in aid of Concern India Foundation) in the 18+ age group category in January 2021.

Cindy has a Master's Degree in English Literature and loves to trek, run and 'catch the sun.' She is married and lives with her husband in Bangalore.